The Adventures of Jo Schmo

Wyatt Burp Rides Again

Greg Trine

Art by Frank W. Dormer

Houghton Mifflin Harcourt
Boston New York

For information about permission to reproduce selections from this book,
write to Permissions, Houghton Mifflin Harcourt Publishing Company,
215 Park Avenue South, New York, New York 10003.

www.hmhco.com

The text of this book is set in Adobe Garamond and King Cool KC Pro.

The Library of Congress has cataloged the hardcover edition as follows:
Trine, Greg.
Wyatt Burp rides again / Greg Trine ; art by Frank W. Dormer.
p. cm. — (The adventures of Jo Schmo ; [2])
Summary: "Fourth-grade superhero Jo Schmo and her drooling dog
Raymond go back in time to stop the infamous and stinky outlaw
Wyatt Burp."— Provided by publisher.
[1. Superheroes—Fiction. 2. Robbers and outlaws—Fiction.
3. Time travel—Fiction. 4. Belching—Fiction. 5. Dogs—Fiction.
6. San Francisco (Calif.)—Fiction. 7. Humorous stories.]
I. Dormer, Frank W., ill. II. Title.
PZ7.T7356Wy 2012
[E]—dc23
2012037273

ISBN 978-0-547-80795-9 hardcover
ISBN 978-0-544-01899-0 paperback

Manufactured in the United States of America
DOC 10 9 8 7 6 5 4 3 2 1
4500462323

For my brother Tim
—G.T.

To the Gungies
—F.D.

contents

1

Bad Guys? What Bad Guys?

Now that the evil Dr. Dastardly was behind bars, all was quiet in San Francisco. Bank robbers stopped robbing, jewel thieves stopped thieving, cat burglars stopped bothering cats . . . and Jo Schmo didn't know what to do with herself. Jo was a crime fighter, and right now there were no crimes to fight. So she went into her backyard and banged on the door of her grandpa's shack. Her grandpa Joe, that is. It can get a little complicated when there are two Joes in one family—Jo and Joe. But more about that later. For now, Jo was banging on the door of . . . Joe.

"Who's there?" the old man yelled.

"It's Jo."

"Joe?"

"No, Jo."

"Oh, *Jo*. Thought I was talking to myself for a second there. Come in, Jo."

Jo opened the front door to the shack and went inside. "I'm bored, Grandpa," Jo began. "Bored with a capital *B*."

This was true. Jo Schmo was bored. Bored with a capital *B*. And a capital *O* and a capital *R* and a capital . . . well, you get the idea. The only thing worse than being bored with a capital *B* was being bored with a capital *X*. If you were bored with a capital *X,* it meant not only were you bored but also you'd lost your ability to spell.

"Bank robbers, car thieves, terrorists . . . I'm not picky, Grandpa," Jo said.

"Not to worry, Jo," Grandpa Joe said. "The bad guys must be taking a break. It happens."

If there was anyone who understood crime fighting—and bad guys—it was Jo's grandpa, who was a retired sheriff. "Thirty-five years in law enforcement, Jo. Trust me. The bad guys are just taking a break. Sooner or later something will happen and—"

"I'll be there to stop them?"

"You'll be there to stop them."

Jo hoped so. Since capturing the evil Dr. Dastardly and his semi-evil assistant, Pete, Jo had been twiddling her thumbs, waiting for the next crime wave.

She'd settle for a crime ripple.

Jo made a fist. "Hope something happens fast, Gramps. My Knuckle Sandwich is starting to get

rusty. If I don't use it soon, I might forget how."
The Knuckle Sandwich was Jo's favorite move.
It was even more effective than the Siberian Ear
Tweak.

Grandpa Joe moaned but said, "You can practice
on me if you like."

"Okay," Jo said. "Put your face over here,
Gramps."

Grandpa Joe leaned closer.

Smack!

Nope. Jo Schmo's Knuckle Sandwich wasn't rusty at all.

Jo left her grandfather's shack and hopped on the Schmomobile. Not every superhero had a supervehicle, but Jo did. The Schmomobile was a supercharged skateboard with a sidecar for her dog and sidekick, Raymond.

"Ready to catch some bad guys, Raymond?" Jo asked.

Raymond gave her a look that said, "Do I like fire hydrants? Are polar bears white? Can fish swim?" Well, you get the idea.

Both Jo and Raymond were in the mood to catch bad guys. If they could find any.

2

A Crime Ripple

It was true that no major crime waves were occurring at that moment in San Francisco, where Jo Schmo lived. But that didn't mean there weren't crime ripples. And sometimes if you have enough crime ripples, they can join together and become a crime wave, which can work its way up to a crime tsunami. Actually, there hadn't been a crime tsunami in San Francisco in years. They were due for one.

But back to the crime ripple.

The crime ripple in question was happening right under Jo Schmo's nose. Before Jo became a superhero, the most popular girls at Prairie Street Elementary School were Gertrude McSlime and her best friend, Betty Sludgefoot.

"I miss being popular," Gertrude said.

"Me too," said Betty. "We need to do something about Jo Schmo."

"And her little dog, too."

"Her dog's name is Too? I thought it was Raymond." Yep. You guessed it. Betty wasn't the sharpest knife in the drawer. She was one taco short of a combination plate. Her elevator didn't go to the top floor. The lights were on but nobody—

Well, you get the idea.

"Yes, Raymond and Jo. They have to go."

The girls were longtime members of the Society of Mean Girls (SMG), which had taught them how to be mean and popular at the same time, but recently Gertrude and Betty had decided to step

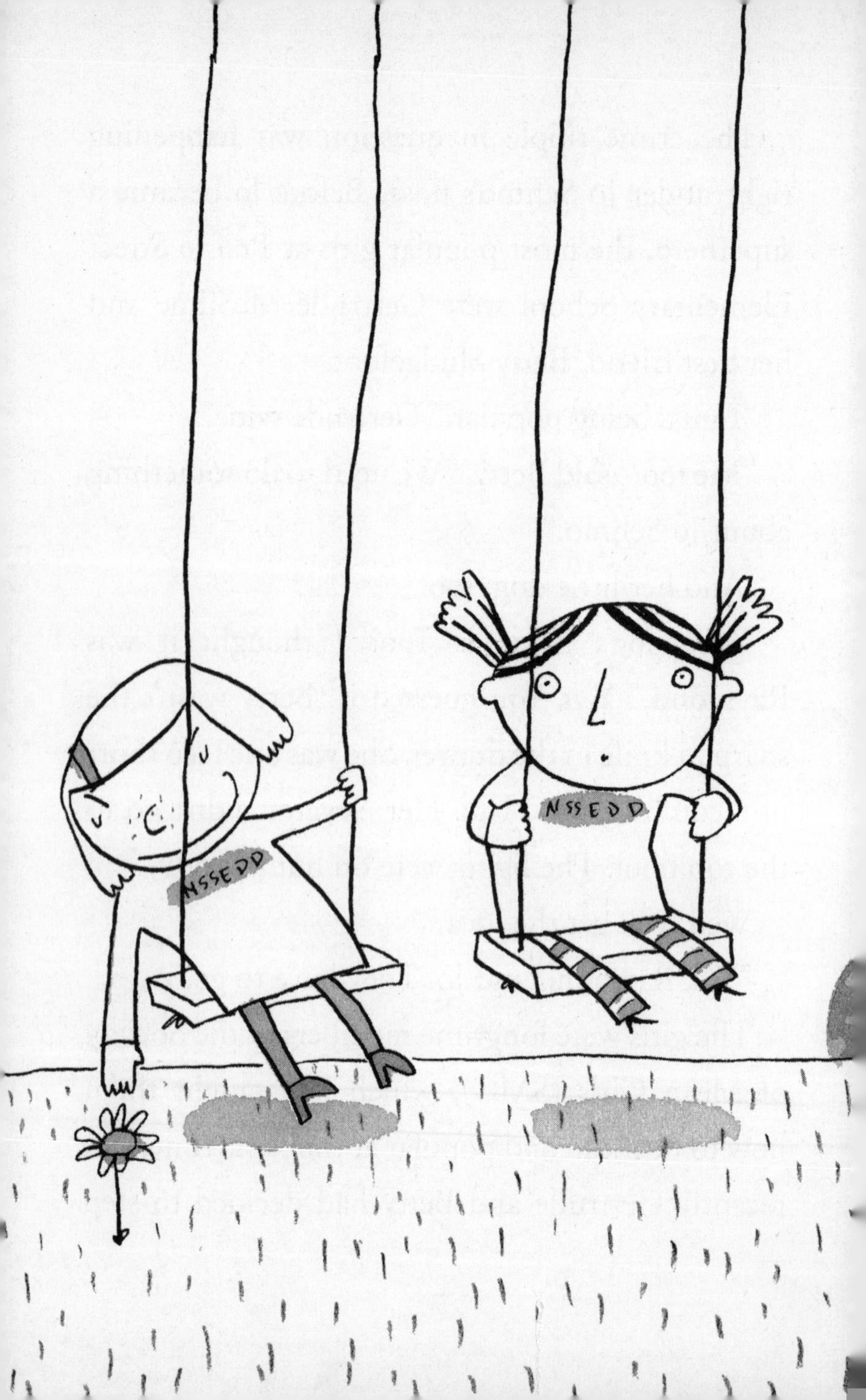
NSSEDD
NSSEDD

up their game. The Society of Mean Girls wasn't enough when you were dealing with a superhero who had a supervehicle.

So Gertrude and Betty had joined the National Society of Supervillains and Evil-Deed Doers (NSSEDD). If Jo Schmo was a superhero (and she was), then Gertrude and Betty had to become supervillains.

"Or my name isn't Gertrude McSlime."

"It's not?" Betty said. Maybe she was *two* tacos short of a combination plate.

"Got any ideas on how to get rid of Jo Schmo?" Gertrude asked her friend.

Betty shook her head. "Ideas? That sounds an awful lot like thinking." Which was not easy to do if your name was Betty Sludgefoot.

"Okay, I'll come up with the plan. But I'm going to need your help."

"I'm in," Betty said.

Jo Schmo had to go, and the two girls wanted her gone as soon as possible.

"I'll be the supervillain," said Gertrude.

"And I'll be the evil-deed doer," said Betty.

Wyatt Burp

Jo Schmo knew nothing of the crime ripple that was going on right under her nose. She was too busy being bored and waiting for a major crime wave to start. This, of course, was her problem. She was so busy looking for something big, she didn't see the small stuff. Like the evil plans of Gertrude McSlime and Betty Sludgefoot.

Gertrude and Betty were in Jo's fourth grade class and were giving Jo their best dirty looks. Dirty looks were how crime ripples began. Gertrude and

Betty would eventually move on to evil thoughts, followed by dastardly deeds, but you had to start somewhere.

But Jo didn't notice the mini crime wave beginning in the back of the room where Gertrude and Betty sat. Jo had her mind on other things.

She glanced at her cell phone. If anything happened, her grandpa Joe would send her a text message about it. But there were no messages on the phone. No bad guys to catch. And Jo didn't see the dirty looks coming her way from Gertrude and Betty.

"All right, class," Mrs. Freep said. "Get out your history books. Today we're going to talk about bad guys."

Jo's ears perked up. Bad guys were her favorite subject. Taking care of evil-deed doers was her life's work. *Easy A,* thought Jo.

In the back of the room, two other sets of ears also perked up. Gertrude McSlime and Betty

Sludgefoot knew a thing or two about bad guys. And they weren't even guys.

Easy A, thought Gertrude.

"During the California gold rush," Mrs. Freep began, "there were many outlaws, including the infamous Wyatt Burp."

All morning long, Mrs. Freep told her class stories of Wyatt Burp and the Hole in the Head Gang. Wyatt Burp, the supervillain. Wyatt Burp, the superburper. He'd once blown the vault doors

off the First National Bank of San Francisco with a single burp, and the smell of what he'd had for breakfast lingered in the air for days.

"I wish I lived back then," Jo whispered to herself. She wouldn't be a bored superhero if she could do battle with Wyatt Burp. "If only I could go back in time."

Jo Schmo wasn't the only one whispering in Mrs. Freep's class. Gertrude leaned toward Betty and said, "Maybe we could burp like Wyatt Burp."

"Jo Schmo wouldn't know what hit her," Betty whispered.

That afternoon the two semi-supervillains from Prairie Street Elementary School joined the National Society for the Advancement of Burping (NSAB).

"If Wyatt Burp could do it, so can we," said Gertrude McSlime.

Betty Sludgefoot agreed.

Strange things were happening in Mrs. Freep's fourth grade class. A superhero was dreaming of going back in time, and a supervillain and a dastardly-deed doer were dreaming about learning how to burp more effectively.

CLANK KABOOM SLAM

While Gertrude McSlime and Betty Sludgefoot were busy joining the National Society for the Advancement of Burping (NSAB), Jo Schmo was getting excited about a certain supervillain who'd wreaked havoc in San Francisco during the California gold rush. Wyatt Burp was one nasty fellow. If only Jo could travel back in time to meet him. She could introduce him to her Knuckle Sandwich.

"Grandpa, Grandpa, Grandpa, Grandpa."
Jo banged on the door of the little shack in her
backyard. "It's me, Jo."

"Oh, Jo. Come in."

Jo went inside. She could barely keep from jump-
ing up and down. She was one excited superhero.
"Do you believe in time travel, Grandpa Joe?"

Grandpa Joe pulled on one bushy eyebrow.
"Time travel?"

"Uh-huh. The bad guys are still on break. But Wyatt Burp is up to no good."

"Wyatt Burp?"

"Yes. He once blew the vault doors off the First National Bank of San Francisco. The smell of what he'd had for breakfast lingered for days. If I can build a time machine, I can go after him."

"Hmm . . ." Grandpa Joe didn't know what to say. *Hmm* would have to do.

Jo couldn't wait for a better answer. She was pretty sure she could build a time machine if she put her mind to it. After all, she'd built her supercharged Schmomobile in a single night. "Wyatt Burp, I'm coming for you," Jo said as she ran for the garage.

Tinker, tinker, tink, rattle, rattle, CLANK. All night long, strange sounds came from Jo Schmo's garage. Not only *tinker, rattle,* and *clank,* but now and then a *snap, crackle,* and *pop.* And sometimes a *KABOOM* and a *SLAM*. If something didn't fit, you made it fit—that was Jo's motto.

Jo's dog, Raymond, looked at her with an expression that said, "Are you sure you know what you're doing?"

"Is ice cream tasty? Is the ocean wet? Do dogs have fleas? Of course I know what I'm doing," Jo said as she swung the sledgehammer.

Tinker, tinker, tink, rattle, rattle, CLANK, KABOOM, SLAM. Jo kept working. When the sun came up, she stood back and looked at her creation. "That's a time machine if I ever saw one," Jo said.

Jo had never seen a time machine. What did she know?

"What do you think, Raymond?"

Raymond's look said, "Beats me. I'm just a dog."

"Trust me. It looks like a time machine. The question is, will it work?"

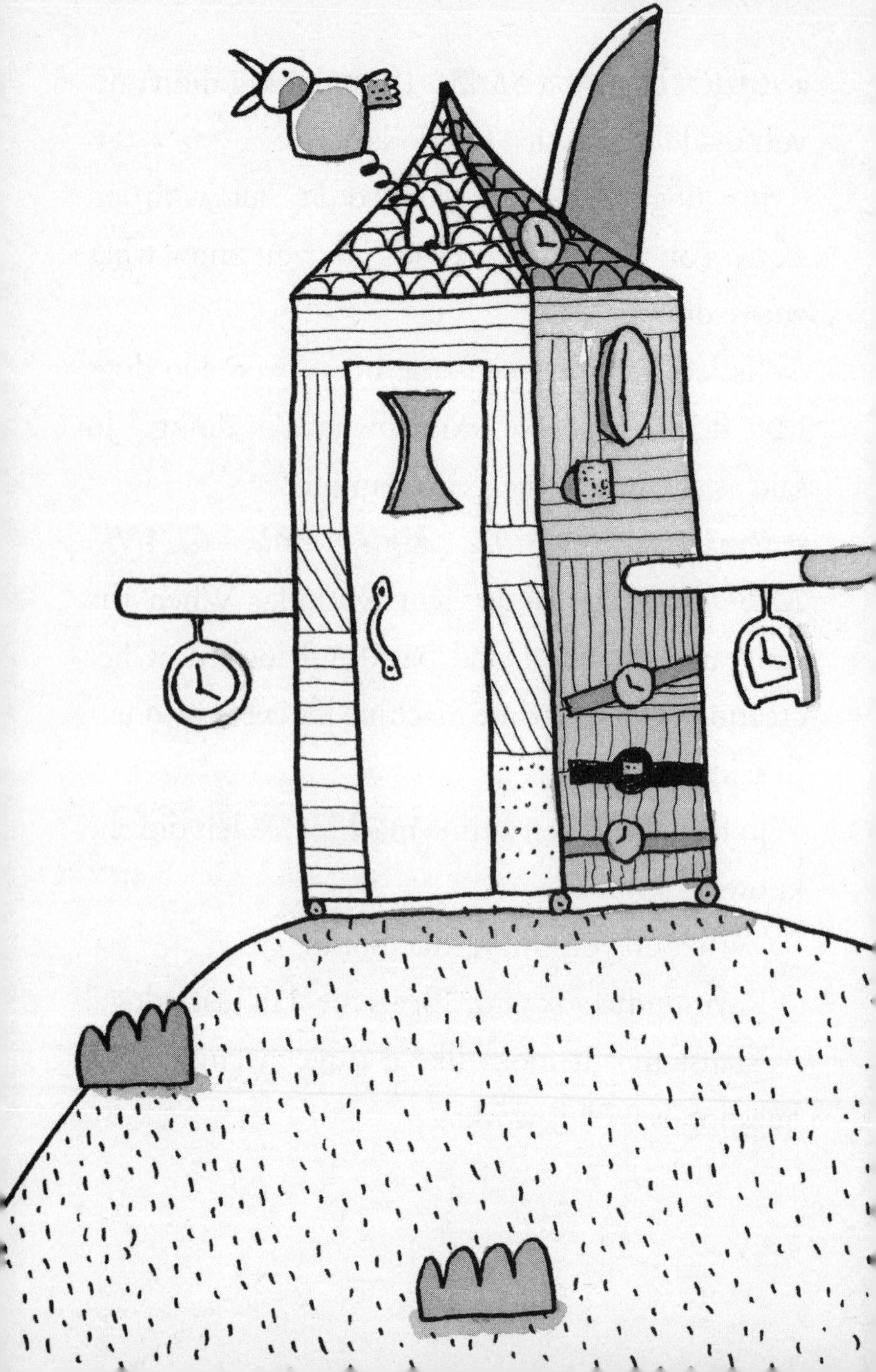

And more important, did they have tasty doggy snacks during the California gold rush? Raymond thought. There was no point in going back in time to catch Wyatt Burp if there were no tasty doggy snacks.

5

The Outhouse . . . uh . . . Time Machine

The time machine didn't look much like a time machine. It looked more like an outhouse with tubes and pipes sticking out. But at least it was big enough for Jo, her dog, and the Schmomobile. If Jo was going back in time to do battle with Wyatt Burp and the Hole in the Head Gang, she would need a vehicle to get around.

Would the time machine work? That was the question.

"And what about those doggy snacks?" Raymond's look said.

"Never mind about that," Jo said. "Climb aboard, Raymond."

Jo put on her superhero cape, then attached Raymond's. Immediately, he began to drool. He couldn't help himself. Something about that cape made him drool like it was going out of style. And it was. Drooling had been out of style for years—even for a dog!

Jo grabbed the Schmomobile and set the dial on the time machine for 1849. "California gold rush, here we come." She pushed the start button, and before you could say "Jo Schmo and company shot back in time to 1849," Jo Schmo and company shot back in time to 1849.

The outhouse . . . uh . . . time machine landed on Crimshaw Avenue (Jo's street) before there was a Crimshaw Avenue. In 1849, it was just a patch of grass overlooking San Francisco Bay.

"Now to find Wyatt Burp. Hop in the Schmomobile, Raymond. Let's go."

While Jo Schmo was busy going back in time, Gertrude McSlime and Betty Sludgefoot were busy concocting an evil scheme to get rid of Jo— and her little dog, Too. Actually, the dog's name was Raymond, not Too, but you get the idea.

The point is, they had to get rid of Jo Schmo, and they had the perfect plan to do it.

During the night, while Jo was busy *tinker*ing, *kaboom*ing, and *clank*ing, Gertrude and Betty hijacked a crane and wrecking ball. They had water balloons as a backup. If the wrecking ball failed, at least they could get Jo Schmo wet. It was a start.

They set up the wrecking ball along Jo's usual route to school and waited. Little did they know that Jo had gone back in time to 1849. It would be more than a hundred and fifty years before Jo showed up. It would be more than a hundred and fifty years before she was even born.

Time travel sure was complicated.

6

The Hole in the Head Gang

Wyatt Burp was not your average, run-of-the-mill outlaw. While most villains used their six-shooters, shotguns, and the occasional stick of dynamite to do their dirty work, Wyatt used his famous sarsaparilla-powered burp. Wyatt's burp was legendary. He once knocked a guy off his horse with a single burp.

Yes, sir, this man could burp. But he didn't work alone. Wyatt was the leader of a pack of desperadoes called the Hole in the Head Gang. They'd wanted to call themselves the Hole in the Wall Gang, but that name was already taken.

Hole in the Head it was. Wyatt didn't care, just as long as he could be the leader.

"What day is it?" Wyatt asked Festus, the Number Two Man in the gang. Festus wasn't second in command. He just smelled bad, which was why they called him the Number Two Man.

"It's Thursday," Festus replied.

Wyatt Burp scratched his chin. "Thursday? Is that Rob-a-Train Day?"

"Wednesday is Rob-a-Train Day," said Festus.

"Rob-a-Bank Day?"

"Monday is Rob-a-Bank Day," said Festus. "And Tuesday is Blow-Something-Up Day."

"I love Tuesdays," Wyatt said with a smile. "What do we do on Thursdays again?"

"Thursdays are Drink-a-Lot-of-Sarsaparilla-and-See-What-Happens Day."

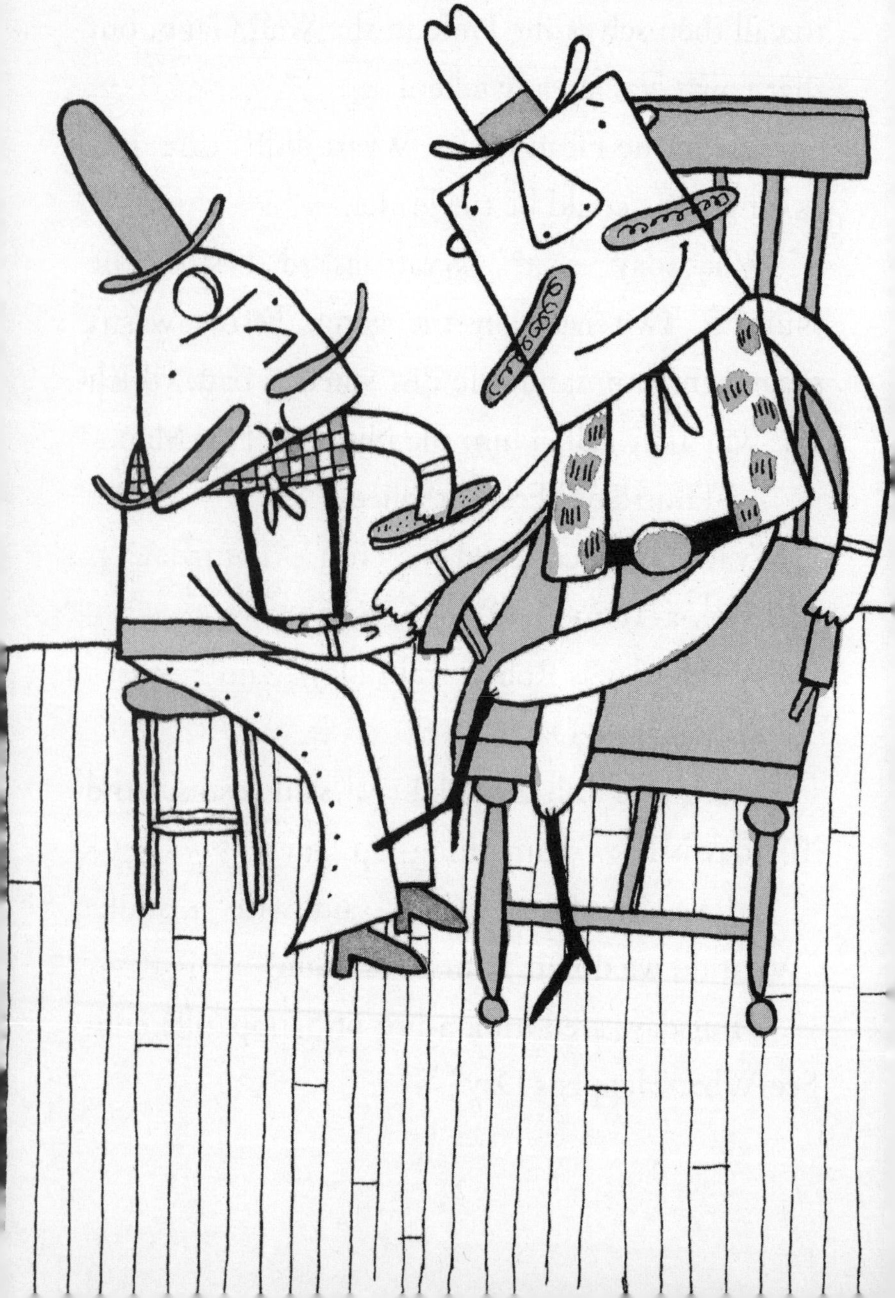

"Sounds good to me," said Wyatt, opening a bottle of his favorite soft drink. Drink-a-Lot-of-Sarsaparilla-and-See-What-Happens Day sounded a whole lot like Blow-Something-Up Day. "I love Thursdays, too."

Festus grinned. He also liked Thursdays. When Wyatt drank a lot of sarsaparilla, anything could happen, which made life in San Francisco very interesting, especially if you were a member of the Hole in the Head Gang. Even if you were the Number Two Man.

"Let's ride," Wyatt Burp said to his gang as he climbed into his saddle.

"Where to?" asked Festus.

"Let's go to town and see what happens." He took another swig of sarsaparilla, preparing for the day.

Yep, Thursdays were just like Tuesdays. Something might blow up, and it wouldn't be from dynamite.

● ● ●

While Wyatt Burp and the Hole in the Head Gang were getting ready for Drink-a-Lot-of-Sarsaparilla-and-See-What-Happens Day, Jo Schmo was speeding through the streets of 1849 San Francisco on the Schmomobile with Raymond in the sidecar drooling like it was going out of style. In 1849, drooling wasn't out of style at all. It was still very popular among dogs. Raymond would fit right in.

Unfortunately, a superhero driving a super-charged skateboard would not fit right in. Jo Schmo was the talk of the town. She pulled to a stop on Market Street and asked a man walking by, "Do you know where I can find Wyatt Burp?"

"Wyatt Burp?"

"Yes."

"The sarsaparilla-drinking, notorious-burping outlaw?"

"Uh-huh."

"The guy who once blew the doors off a bank

vault with a single burp, and the smell of what he had for breakfast lingered in the area for days?"

"That's him."

"Never heard of the guy."

7

BuRRRRRRRP!

This is not going to be easy, Jo thought. *How am I going to find Wyatt Burp and introduce him to my Knuckle Sandwich? Or my Siberian Ear Tweak, for that matter?* Jo didn't know. She gunned the engine of the Schmomobile and raced along Market Street. If Wyatt Burp was taking a day off from evil-deed doing, she would be very disappointed.

"Got any ideas, Raymond?" Jo asked her dog.

Raymond gave her a look that said, "Don't bother me; I'm thinking of doggy snacks." He was drooling more than ever now. Good thing it was still in style. As the Schmomobile sped along, Raymond laid down a path of dog drool a mile long.

Where was Wyatt Burp? According to Mrs. Freep, Wyatt Burp and the Hole in the Head Gang wreaked havoc in San Francisco in 1849.

But there was no sign of him.

Jo kept an eye peeled. She sniffed the air for the smell of Wyatt Burp's breakfast. Smelling breakfast would tell her she was on the right track. Either that or it meant she was in the restaurant district.

Jo kept looking . . . and smelling. So far, nothing. Just crowded streets full of prospectors, and—

Suddenly, thunder roared across the sky!

Jo looked up. There wasn't a dark cloud in sight.

And right then she smelled something. "Bacon," Jo said. "Do you smell it, Raymond?"

"Bacon!" Raymond's look said. He knew he liked 1849.

Jo kept looking up. "Either someone's cooking breakfast or Wyatt Burp is in the area."

Thunder crashed again. Only it sounded more like *BURRRRRRRP!* This time it knocked Jo and Raymond off the Schmomobile. And they smelled not only bacon but also sausage and eggs.

Wyatt Burp, thought Jo as she picked herself up off the ground.

I'm staying in 1849 forever, thought Raymond.

"Let's go, Raymond."

"Yes, let's," Raymond's look said.

They hopped back on the Schmomobile and turned off Market Street just in time for—

BURRRRRRRP!

The blast threw Jo and Raymond into the side

34

of a building. And there stood Wyatt Burp, Festus the Number Two Man, and the rest of the Hole in the Head Gang.

"Ha-ha! Pardon me, little sister," Wyatt said. He was sorry to knock over a nine-year-old girl and her dog. But he wasn't *that* sorry. "Ha-ha!"

"That's the worst evil laugh I've ever heard," Jo whispered.

Raymond gave her a look that said, "Never mind that. Where's the bacon?" Raymond was all for catching bad guys, just not during snack time.

Jo got to her feet. "Stop in the name of—"

Stop in the name of what? This was the hardest part of superhero work—figuring out what to add after "Stop in the name of." Stop in the name of a fourth grade girl and her little dog, too? Stop in the name of time travel? Stop in the name of "No one wants to smell your breakfast"?

While Jo was trying to figure out what to add after "Stop in the name of," Wyatt Burp and the Hole in the Head Gang got away.

"Drat!" yelled Jo.

"Double drat!" the look on Raymond's face said. He really wanted that bacon.

Burping Practice

Gertrude McSlime and Betty Sludgefoot didn't know that Jo Schmo had gone back in time. They were busy setting up the crane and wrecking ball at the end of Crimshaw Avenue and waiting for Jo to pass by so they could squash her like a bug. Bug-squashing was one of Betty's favorite pastimes. She had never squashed a Jo Schmo before, but she was very open to new experiences.

While they waited for Jo, the two girls practiced their burping. If Wyatt Burp could do it, so could they. After all, they were now members of the National Society for the Advancement of Burping (NSAB), an organization founded way back in 1849 by Wyatt himself.

Gertrude read from the NSAB brochure. "It says here that Wyatt Burp got his burping power by drinking mass quantities of sarsaparilla."

"Sarsaparilla? What's that?"

"It's a soft drink from a long time ago."

"Where can we get our hands on some?"

Gertrude shook her head. "No need. We'll use the modern stuff. Coke, Dr Pepper, Sprite. Mix them together and see what happens. We'll be burping like Wyatt Burp in no time, or my name isn't Gertrude McSlime."

"It's not?" And all this time, Betty had thought her best friend's name was Gertrude McSlime.

"Never mind. Let's go get something to help us burp more effectively. So we can burp—"

"Like a lumberjack?" Betty asked.

"Like Wyatt Burp, the best burper of all time."

The two girls climbed down off the crane and ran for the nearest convenience store. Gertrude was so excited that she let out an evil laugh. "Jo Schmo won't know what hit her. If we miss with the wrecking ball, we'll burp her to death."

"Death by burping?" Betty made a face. "I've never heard of such a thing."

"Me neither. But don't forget, Wyatt Burp once blew the vault doors off the First National Bank of San Francisco. Those doors could have landed on someone and squashed him."

"I love squashing things," Betty said.

"I know."

Back at the crane, Gertrude McSlime and Betty Sludgefoot began mixing together different soft drinks and testing the combinations. The more carbonation the better.

BURRRRRRRP!

"Not bad," Betty said. She was proud to be a member of the National Society for the Advancement of Burping.

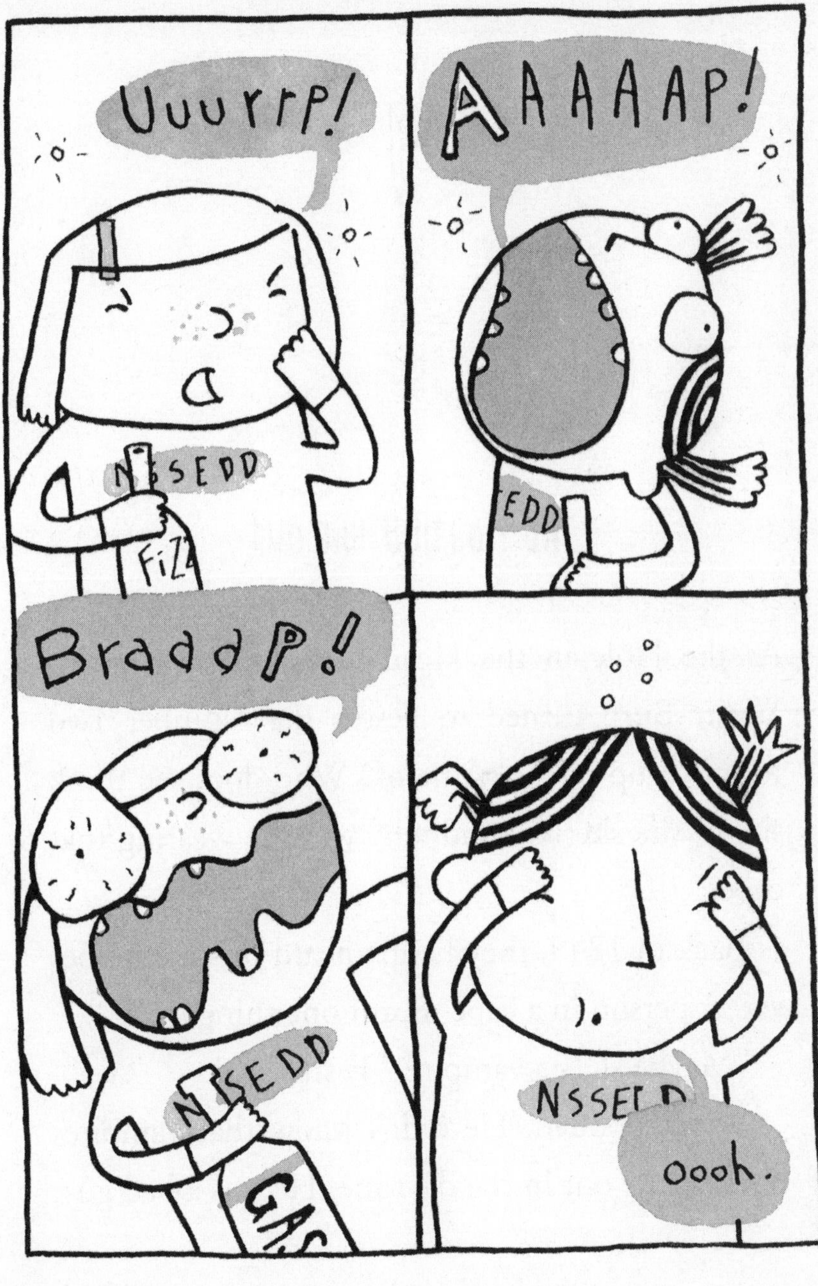
Uuurrp!
NSSEDD
FiZZ
AAAAAP!
EDD
BradddP!
NSSEDD
GAS
NSSEED
Oooh.

9

The Floating Hideout

As the Hole in the Head Gang galloped away, Wyatt Burp turned to Festus the Number Two Man. "Stop in the name of? Who does she think she is, the sheriff? And why was she wearing that cape?"

Back in 1849, they hadn't heard of superheroes yet. A person in a cape meant one thing.

"Maybe she's a vampire," Festus said.

Wyatt nodded. He didn't know that vampires never came out in the daytime. He was a bad guy, not an expert in vampires. "We better keep an eye out for that little girl in the red cape."

"And her little dog, too?"

"Yes. The dog was wearing a cape as well."

"And drooling like it was going out of style."

"Fortunately, this is 1849. Drooling is very much in style."

"If you say so." Festus the Number Two Man was known to drool now and then himself. But it was usually when he was in the presence of an attractive woman.

With Wyatt Burp and the Hole in the Head Gang gone, so was the smell of what Wyatt had had for breakfast. Raymond looked at Jo with an expression that said, "I no longer smell bacon and it's all your fault."

"Not to worry, Raymond," Jo said. "Let's go."

The Schmomobile could go from zero to sixty in 4.3 seconds. Wyatt Burp and his gang were on horses. Jo could run them down in less than a minute.

If she could figure out which way they went.

Jo and Raymond hopped on the Schmomobile and raced down the street. "Keep an ear perked, Raymond," Jo said. "Listen for something that sounds like thunder."

Raymond gave her a look that said, "*You* keep an ear perked for something that sounds like thunder. I'll keep my nose perked for something that smells like bacon."

"That'll work," Jo said.

The Schmomobile raced through the streets of San Francisco, Jo's cape flapping behind her, and Raymond drooling even more than before. *Bacon,* he thought, *breakfast of champions . . . breakfast of superheroes.*

Wyatt Burp brought his galloping horse to a stop

near the wharf and looked out at San Francisco Bay, which was filled with abandoned ships. The ships had come from all over the world, filled with prospectors headed for the California goldfields. Many of the ships were now unoccupied.

"I've always wanted a floating hideout," Wyatt said. "Gang, huddle up."

Festus the Number Two Man and the rest of the gang gathered around their leader.

"Boys, it has come to my attention that we're being pursued by a vampire. A mini vampire, but still, a bite on the neck is a bite on the neck. What do you say we take one of these ships to the other side of the bay and make plans?"

"Aye!" cheered the gang.

"Who knows anything about sailing?"

No one said a word. They were outlaws, not sailors.

10

Super Dog Paddle

"Hoist that heavy thing!" Wyatt Burp commanded.

"You mean the anchor?" Festus the Number Two Man asked. Festus wasn't a sailor, but even he knew what an anchor was.

Once the anchor was pulled up, the gang raised the sails, and soon the ship was headed across the bay. There was not much wind, but with Wyatt on board, they could create their own. Wind, that is.

"Here, drink some more sarsaparilla, boss,"

Festus said. When Wyatt finished a bottle, Festus added, "Okay, let her rip."

"BURRRRRRRP!"

With a blast of hot air—and the smell of bacon—the ship picked up speed and sailed away from the wharf.

"BURRRRRRRP!"

"Did you hear that, Raymond?" The Schmomobile raced toward the waterfront, capes flying and dog drool trailing behind.

Raymond gave her a look that said, "More important, I smelled it. *Bacon!* Faster, Jo. I want snacks."

Moments later, the two superheroes arrived at the wharf, just in time for—

"BURRRRRRRP!"

Jo Schmo looked out across the bay. "There they are!" She pointed to a ship sailing away from them. There wasn't much wind, but burp power seemed to be working just fine.

And the smell was making Raymond crazy.

"Down, boy," Jo said to her dog.

Raymond didn't feel like lying down, not when there was bacon to be had.

The problem was that Jo and Raymond couldn't

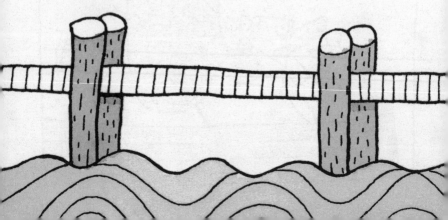

sail a large ship by themselves, and besides, wouldn't that be stealing? Stealing was a crime. How could a superhero do such a thing? And what would her retired-sheriff grandfather have to say about that?

Also, Jo Schmo didn't know how to swim. If she jumped in the water, she'd sink like . . . a heavy thing. She stood on the shore, watching the ship sail farther and farther away.

Jo looked at her dog. "Do you know how to swim, Raymond?"

"Do I hate fleas?" Raymond's look said. "Does bacon smell good? Do I want some *right now?*" He really did want some right now. Sooner, if possible.

"Follow me." Jo ran along the waterfront,

looking for a boat small enough for the two of them to handle. They wouldn't steal it—they'd just borrow it for a while.

"There!" It was a small wooden rowboat, perfect for a superhero. Jo climbed into the boat and untied it from the dock. She held on to Raymond's front paws while the rest of him dangled in the water. "Dog-paddle, boy."

"Brrrrrrrrr," Raymond's look said.

"Do you want bacon or don't you?" Jo asked. She didn't have to say another word. Bacon was exactly what Raymond wanted. Eggs and sausage, too, but bacon was his all-time favorite.

With the thought of bacon in his head, Raymond dog-paddled like he never had before. The little rowboat sped away from the dock in pursuit of the burp-powered ship and the Hole in the Head Gang.

11

"MWah-ha—BURRRRRRRP—ha!"

You may be asking yourself, "What was going on in modern times while Raymond was busy dog-paddling back in 1849?" If you're not asking that, go ahead and ask.

Thanks for asking.

While Raymond was busy dog-paddling back in 1849, Gertrude McSlime and Betty Sludgefoot were sitting in the wrecking-ball machine, waiting for Jo Schmo to walk by so they could squash her

like a bug. As you know, squashing bugs was one of Betty Sludgefoot's favorite pastimes.

While they sat and waited for Jo, they mixed up different combinations of soft drinks and kept working on their burps. If Wyatt Burp could do it, so could they. Or so they thought.

BURRRRRRP!

"Not bad," Gertrude said to Betty.

To be honest, it *was* kind of bad. It wasn't exactly

a Wyatt Burp–caliber burp. It was more like a Betty Sludgefoot burp. It couldn't blow the doors off anything. It was more like the wind created by a passing butterfly.

But the two girls didn't care. Their burps seemed loud enough to wake the dead, and that was all that mattered. If you couldn't blow the doors off things, you could at least be loud. Besides, the wrecking ball would do the real work. Jo Schmo wouldn't know what hit her until it was too late.

Just thinking about it made Gertrude smile. She threw back her head and let out an evil laugh. *"Mwah-ha—BURRRRRRRP—ha!"*

An evil-laugh-and-burp combo. Even Wyatt Burp would be impressed.

The girls waited and waited. Then they waited. And after they waited, they . . . waited. But there was no sign of Jo Schmo.

"Maybe we should do a practice swing with the wrecking ball," Betty suggested.

"Good idea," said Gertrude. "What's our target?"

"See the bug on that wall?"

"Okay, here goes."

If they could hit a bug on a wall, they could hit a Jo Schmo.

Gertrude pulled a few levers, and the wrecking ball swung toward the bug—

CRASH!

"Did I hit the bug?" Gertrude asked.

Betty shook her head. "Not sure, but that building is history."

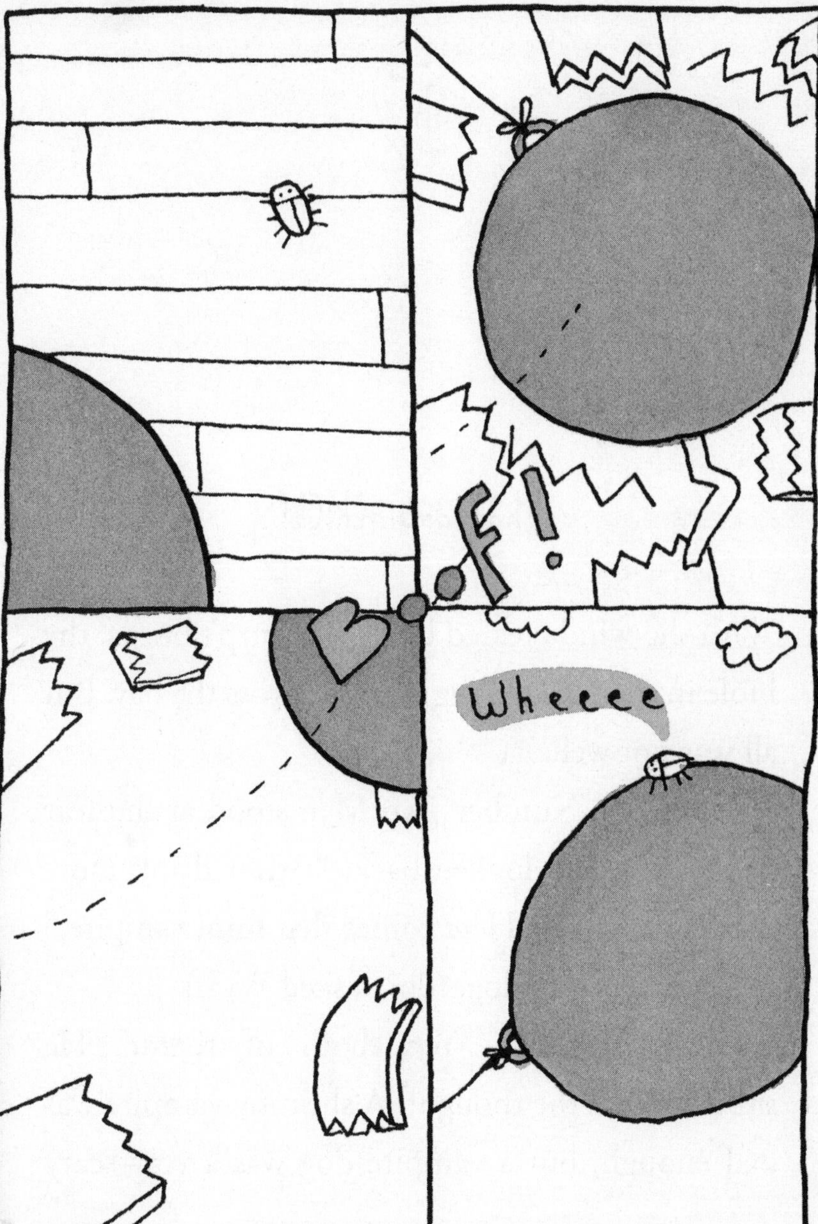
f!
Wheeee

12

That-a-Sidekick!

With the wind created by Wyatt Burp's burps, the Hole in the Head Gang headed across the bay. But all was not well.

Festus the Number Two Man stood at the rear of the ship and looked back. "Better drink more sarsaparilla, boss. Here comes that mini vampire."

"And her little dog, too?" asked Wyatt.

Festus nodded. "Yep, both of them." He shuddered at the thought. A shrimpy vampire was bad enough, but a vampire dog was a very scary thing. "More burps, boss. I think they're gaining on us."

Festus was right—they were gaining on them. Raymond was an expert dog paddler. He was, after all, a dog. But he was also a superhero's sidekick. He had superpowers, so he could not only drool like it was going out of style but also do a super dog paddle. And dog paddling was very much in style, even in 1849.

The little rowboat occupied by Jo Schmo and powered by Raymond sped across the bay. "That-a-boy," said Jo. "Keep it up, Raymond."

Raymond kept paddling.

Meanwhile, Wyatt drank more sarsaparilla and kept burping. Single burps, double burps, and a few triple burps thrown in just for the heck of it.

And then something happened. A bank of fog rolled into the bay. A fog thick as quicksand—maybe thicker.

"If we can make it to the fog, she'll never find

us," Wyatt said. And with that, he burped even more.

"Almost there, boss," said Festus the Number Two Man.

Jo Schmo didn't see the bank of fog roll in. She had her back turned because she was holding the front paws of Raymond while he paddled.

But Raymond saw the fog. He gave Jo a look that said, "Uh-oh."

Jo turned around to see what he was uh-ohing about. The ship occupied by the Hole in the Head

Gang and powered by Wyatt and his sarsaparilla disappeared into the fog.

"Uh-oh," Jo said. "Don't tell me they just disappeared into the fog."

Raymond's look said, "Okay, I won't tell you. But what do we do now?"

"Keep paddling, Raymond. I'll think of something."

Jo had once gotten an A in thinking, in Mrs. Freep's class. If anyone could come up with something, Jo could. But right now she was all out of ideas.

13

Thick as a Milk Shake

"Ha-ha! We're safe," Wyatt Burp said. "Ha-ha!" He didn't care that he had the worst evil laugh the world had ever known. The important thing was that they were safe inside the fog, and the mini vampire and her little dog, too, wouldn't be able to find them.

But just in case, Wyatt passed out scarves to the members of his gang.

"It's just fog, boss," Festus the Number Two Man said.

"I don't care about the fog," Wyatt said. He pointed behind the ship. "There's still a vampire out there, and—"

"A bite on the neck is a bite on the neck?"

"Exactly," Wyatt said. "Cover your necks, boys."

Wyatt wrapped a scarf around his neck and kept burping into the sails. With all the fog, he couldn't see where they were going. But somewhere behind them there was a mini vampire. And a bite on the neck, even a mini one, might not be a whole lot of fun.

"Keep an eye peeled, boys. She might be closer than we think."

You might be asking yourself, "If Jo Schmo is a superhero, she must have x-ray vision, so why can't she see through the fog?"

Good question.

The fact is, Jo's cape was something she inherited, and it came with a set of instructions. Jo hadn't yet read the chapter on x-ray vision. She didn't know how to use it. Besides, maybe it didn't work in fog. She'd have to wait until she got back to modern times to find out.

If she made it back to modern times.

"Keep paddling, Raymond. We're almost there."

Almost to the fog, that is.

Moments later, they entered the fog, which was now thicker than quicksand—it was more like a chocolate milk shake.

"I can't see a thing," Jo said.

Raymond's look said, "More important, I can't smell bacon."

The reason Raymond couldn't smell bacon was that Wyatt Burp had realized that although his burping was making them go faster, the sound was giving them away. So was the smell. Best not to burp at all and let the fog do its job.

This was the plan of Wyatt Burp and the Hole in the Head Gang. They were adrift in the fog. No one could see a thing, which was perfect. If they couldn't see, neither could Jo and her little vampire dog, too.

"Ha-ha!" Wyatt said under his breath. "She'll never find us now." But he gave his neck another wrap with the scarf, just in case. Mini vampires couldn't be trusted.

14

The Plot Thickens . . . and So Does the Fog

A few seconds later, Jo's rowboat, powered by the dog-paddling Raymond, entered the fog, which had grown even thicker. Thicker than a chocolate milk shake. It was now more like concrete.

Yes, this stuff was thick. So thick in fact that Jo could no longer see Raymond, even though she was holding his front paws.

"You're still there, aren't you, boy? I feel something like paws . . . just want to be sure."

Raymond gave her a look that said, "I feel something like human hands. I'm hoping it's you."

The fog was so thick that Jo couldn't see the look on Raymond's face.

"Raymond?"

Raymond decided he'd have to use his dog voice. *"Ruff!"*

"I'll take that as a yes," Jo said. "Keep paddling. We've got to be close."

Festus the Number Two Man stood at the rear of the ship, staring back into the fog. "Did you hear that, Wyatt?"

"I heard it," Wyatt said.

"A vampire-dog bark if I've ever heard one."

Festus had never heard one. What did he know?

"Hard to starboard!" Wyatt ordered, and the person at the ship's wheel turned it hard to the right.

You may be asking yourself how Wyatt Burp knew what *starboard* meant if he didn't know the word *anchor*. I know . . . go figure.

In any case, the ship turned to the right, and when it did, it kicked up a little wave, which made a splash, and the sound of the splash carried across the water to Jo Schmo.

"We've got them now, Raymond," Jo said, and she moved her dog slightly so that the rowboat turned to the right.

By now the fog had lifted just enough for Jo to see Raymond's face. He gave her a look that said, "I don't smell bacon. What's the point?"

"The point is that Wyatt Burp and his gang are havoc-wreakers, and we're going to stop their havoc-wreaking."

Raymond didn't care about havoc-wreaking. He'd much rather pursue bacon. But he went along with Jo's plan. He was, after all, a sidekick. It was his job to help the superhero in charge. He was also man's (and girl's) best friend, and with that thought, he dog-paddled just a little harder. Bacon or no bacon, he had a job to do.

And right then something went *THUNK!*

A *THUNK* usually indicates that something

solid has just hit something else solid, like, for example, a rowboat hitting the back of a ship.

Raymond gave Jo a look that said, "Is it just me, or was that a *THUNK*?"

"That was definitely a *THUNK*!" Jo said.

The fog had lifted even more, so when Jo turned around, she could see the ship occupied by Wyatt Burp and the Hole in the Head Gang.

"Time to go to work, Raymond." She yanked her dog out of the water and tossed him onto the ship. Then she scampered up after him.

"Stop in the name of—"

While she was pondering what to add after "Stop in the name of," Wyatt Burp took a swig of sarsaparilla and did what he did best.

BURRRRRRRP!

The blast tossed Jo and Raymond off the back of the ship and into the bay. And Jo Schmo, who couldn't swim, sank beneath the waves.

Smashing Practice

Back in modern times, Gertrude McSlime and Betty Sludgefoot had no idea that Jo Schmo was sinking like a brick to the bottom of San Francisco Bay. They were too busy staring at the building they had just demolished with the wrecking ball. One of Betty's favorite pastimes was squashing bugs, but she found she liked squashing buildings just as much.

"Is it okay to have two favorite pastimes?" Betty asked.

"Absolutely," said Gertrude.

"Great. How about we smash another building?"

Gertrude shook her head. "How about we don't? This wrecking ball is for squashing Jo Schmo, remember?"

"Practice makes perfect," Betty said.

"Good point." Gertrude yanked on a few levers, and—

SMASH! Gertrude's aim was right on target. Another building bit the dust.

"Time for another evil-laugh-and-burping session," Gertrude said with a smile.

"I agree," said Betty. "Pour the soda."

Moments later, both girls took a swig, and—

"Mwah-ha—BURRRRRRRP—ha!"

"Now if only Jo Schmo would show up, this day would be perfect," Betty said.

Gertrude agreed. If only Jo Schmo would show up . . .

But Jo didn't show up. Time clicked by. Actually, it ticked by. And tocked, for that matter. The point is that there was no sign of Jo Schmo.

Gertrude and Betty decided to stop smashing buildings while they waited. People were starting to look at them funny. Which made sense, since some of them had just become homeless. Or at least buildingless.

Gertrude and Betty waited, saving the wrecking ball for Jo. They also saved their burps. And the water balloons.

"Where is she?" Gertrude wondered.

"I don't know," complained Betty, "but I'm getting bored."

"Bored with a capital *B*?"

Betty nodded.

"At least you're not bored with a capital *X*. If you're bored with a capital *X*, it means not only are you bored but—"

"I lost my ability to spell?"

"Exactly."

To be honest, Betty had never had much of an ability to spell. She was too busy being a mean girl to concentrate on her schoolwork. After all, she was a future supervillain . . . a girl had to have her priorities.

And so the girls sat and waited. Then they waited. And after they waited, they . . . waited.

Gertrude pulled a deck of cards from her pocket and dealt them out. The two girls played three rounds of crazy eights, four rounds of blackjack, and then moved on to go fish.

"Got any threes?" Gertrude asked.

"Go fish."

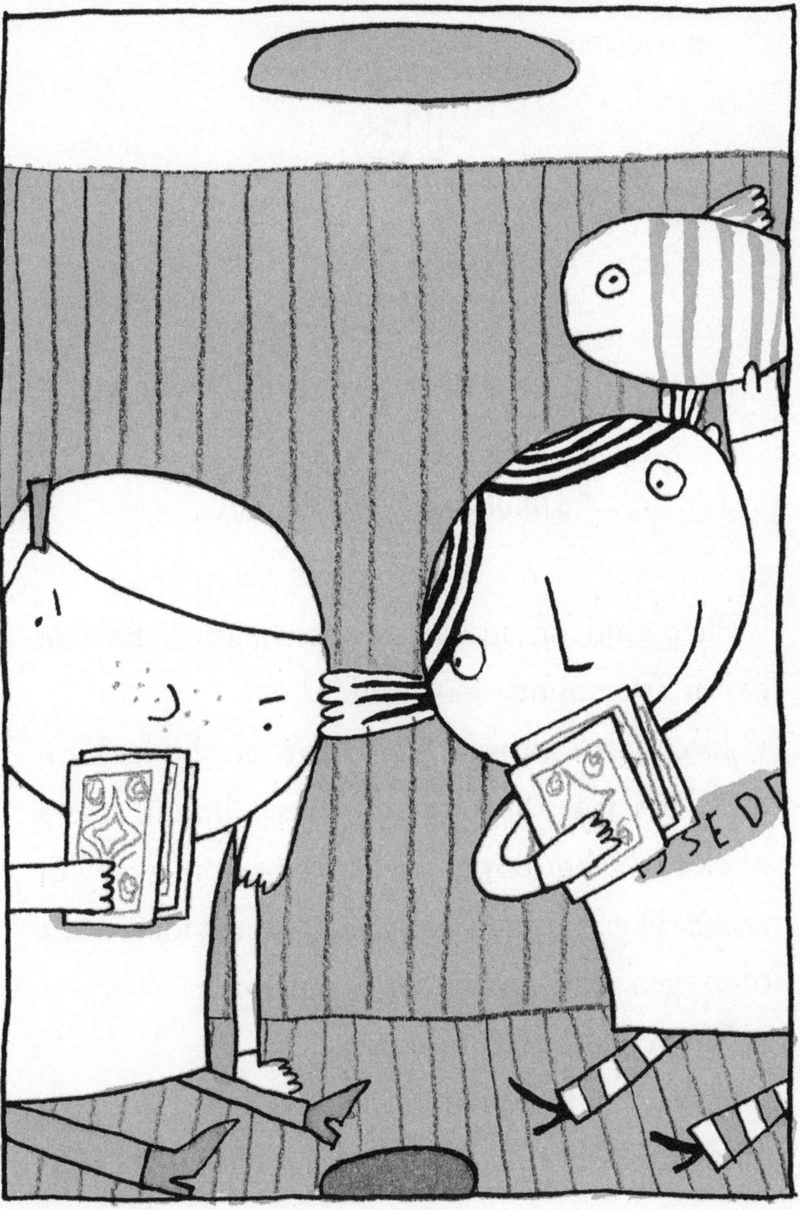

16

Raymond to the Rescue

"What kind of superhero doesn't know how to swim?" Raymond's look said.

Jo couldn't answer. She didn't see the look on her dog's face. She was too busy sinking like a brick to the bottom of the bay to be bothered with things like reading Raymond's expressions. Lack of oxygen tends to do that to a person.

Deeper and deeper she sank.

It was up to Raymond to save her. He didn't know CPR, but he did do a mean dog paddle. In fact, he did a superhero one. He dove beneath the waves with an expression that said, "Don't worry, Jo. I'm coming."

Down he went, one dog paddle at a time. When he reached Jo, both of them were nearly out of air. Jo flapped her arms in a desperate attempt to get to the surface. It wasn't working. She was a superhero, not a swimmer.

"BONK"

And that's when Raymond got an idea. He gave her a look that said, "Maybe you can't swim, but aren't you a superhero? Can't you fly?"

That's right! Jo thought. She *was* a superhero. She *could* fly. Flying was just a matter of saying the magic words, and the magic words were *sponge cake*.

"Sponge cake!" Jo said, grabbing hold of Raymond.

Unfortunately, she was underwater. What came out of her mouth was something more like "Blubby!" Saying *blubby* wouldn't cause anyone to fly, even if you were an airline pilot.

Jo tried again: "Flubby!" *Flubby* was even worse than *blubby*. Although it did rhyme, and you had to give a person credit for rhyming, especially a drowning person.

Drowning person!

Jo sank deeper into the bay.

Time for Raymond to take things into his own paws. Instead, he used his teeth. He grabbed Jo by the cape and dog-paddled toward the surface. He wanted to give her a look that said, "Hold on, Jo, we'll be there in a jiffy," but his face was a little occupied at the moment.

A few seconds later they burst above the surface, both of them gasping for air. When Jo caught her breath, she gave her dog's neck a squeeze and said, "Thanks, Raymond. You're the best sidekick a superhero ever had. Ready, boy? Let's fly." She wrapped her arms around him and added, "Sponge cake!"

Jo and Raymond lifted out of the water.

"Sponge cake!" Jo said again.

They rose even further.

"Sponge cake!" she said a third time. And before you could say "Jo Schmo and her dog were flying like a couple of real superheroes," Jo Schmo and her dog were flying like a couple of real superheroes.

You might be asking yourself, "If Jo Schmo could fly, why did she waste so much time with that rowboat?" I know . . . go figure.

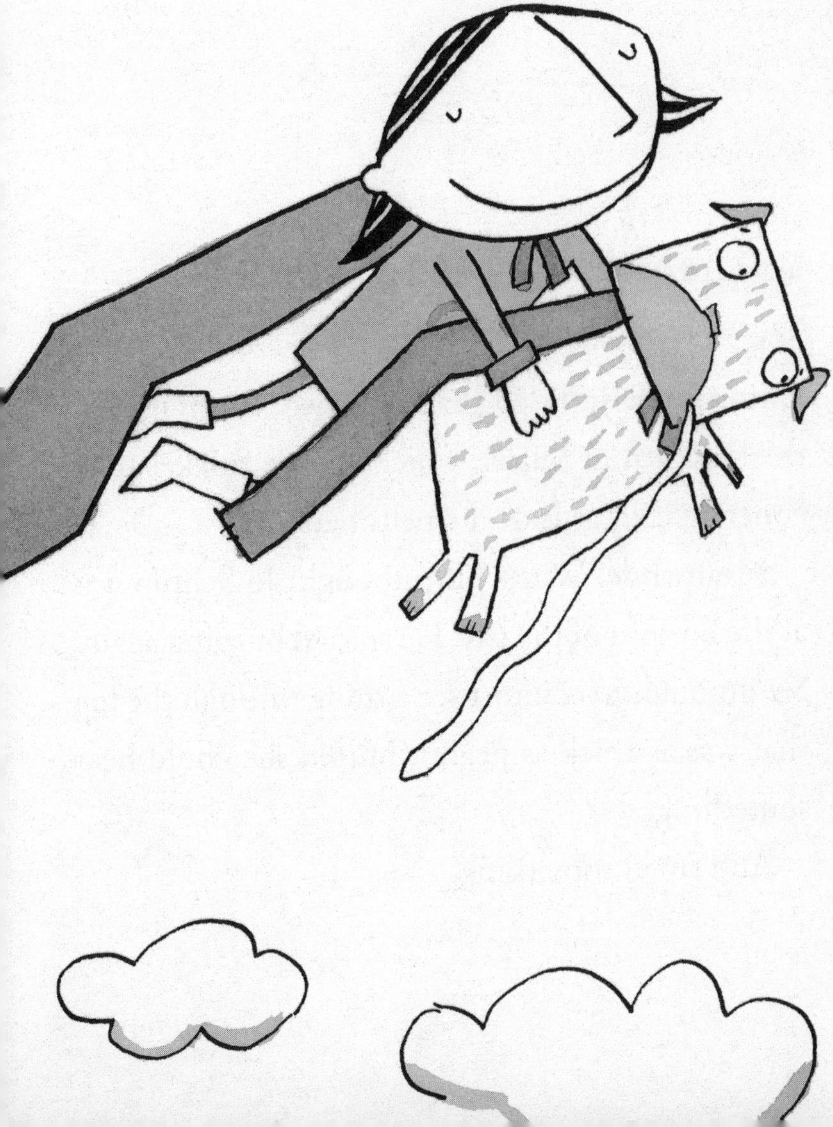

Fog as Thick as Peanut Butter

Unfortunately, the fog had returned. It was now as thick as peanut butter, which is even thicker than concrete. But at least it smells better.

Meanwhile, Wyatt Burp thought Jo Schmo was at the bottom of the bay. He started burping again. So although Jo couldn't see a thing through the fog that was as thick as peanut butter, she could hear something.

And smell something.

Bacon! Raymond thought, and he fell in love with 1849 all over again.

Jo flew toward the sound of the burping and the smell of the bacon, not to mention the smell of sausage and eggs.

BURRRRRRRP!

Jo knew she was close. The burps were getting louder and louder. Moments later, Jo and Raymond flew straight into the ship's mast and fell—*plunk*—onto the deck.

The fog was too thick for anyone to see this happen, but that didn't mean they didn't hear it.

"Is it just me or did something just go *plunk*?" Festus the Number Two Man asked.

"I heard it," Wyatt said, and he wrapped his scarf tighter around his neck. "That mini vampire is back."

"Don't you mean 'Curses! That mini vampire is back'?"

That's exactly what Wyatt meant, but he was too worried about his neck to think straight and use the proper bad-guy words like "Curses!"

"What's the plan, boss?"

"No one can stand up to my burps," Wyatt said proudly. "I once blew the vault doors off a bank. I can take care of a little girl in a cape."

"And her little dog, too?"

"Both of them." Wyatt took another swig of sarsaparilla.

Right then the fog lifted just enough to reveal Jo and Raymond.

Wyatt took aim. *BURRRRRRRP!*

Just as before, the blast tossed Jo and Raymond off the ship. Raymond didn't mind getting wet again. He was too busy enjoying the smell of his favorite breakfast meat.

But before they hit the water, Jo remembered the magic words. "Sponge cake!" she called out. This time, instead of splashing into the bay and sinking like a brick, she held on to Raymond and they hovered just above the surface.

"His burps are too powerful," Jo said. "Got any ideas, Raymond?"

Raymond gave her a look that said, "Don't look at me. I'm just a dog."

By now the fog, which had formerly been as thick as peanut butter, concrete, a chocolate milk shake, and quicksand, had completely lifted, and Jo saw—

"An island," she said. "Let's go build a fire and dry out. I think better when I'm dry."

"Sounds like a plan," Raymond's look said.

18

Jo Has a Plan

"Hey, isn't that an island?" Festus the Number Two Man asked.

"That's exactly what it is," Wyatt replied. "I'm getting tired of this floating hideout. What do you say we take a floating-hideout break?"

"Sounds good to me," said Festus the Number Two Man, who was beginning to feel seasick. So were most of the Hole in the Head Gang. They were bad guys, not sailors—they much preferred dry land.

"Hard to starboard," Wyatt called out, and the ship headed to the island.

This, of course, was the very same island that Jo Schmo had discovered. While Wyatt Burp and the Hole in the Head Gang were sailing to one side of the island, Jo and Raymond were sitting before a

raging fire on the other side, making plans. Or at least getting dry. Making plans would come later.

Darkness had come to the island occupied by a superhero and her dog on one side and a pack of havoc-wreakers on the other.

Jo and Raymond were now completely dry.

"Okay, Raymond, where does Wyatt Burp get his burping power?" Jo asked.

Raymond gave her a look that said, "Sarsaparilla. Even I know that, and I'm just a dog."

"Right. So if we get rid of the sarsaparilla, Wyatt would burp just like anyone else."

That was the plan. It's amazing what you can come up with when you're dry. And now that it was night, it was a perfect time to get the job done.

"Let's go, Raymond." Jo grabbed hold of her dog. "Sponge cake!" she yelled, and the two of them took off.

They rose above the island and spotted the ship on the other side. The members of the Hole in the Head Gang were now onshore, sitting before a huge fire. And there was Wyatt Burp himself. Next to him sat a large crate full of sarsaparilla bottles.

Jo and Raymond flew silently, and then they

dropped into the woods just outside Wyatt's camp. "Are you cold, Raymond?" she whispered to her dog.

Raymond gave her a look that said, "Nope. It's a warm night."

"So why are they all wearing scarves?"

"I know. What kind of bad guys are they?" Raymond's look said.

Jo Schmo and Raymond waited at the edge of the woods until every member of the Hole in the Head Gang was sound asleep.

"Follow me," Jo whispered.

They tiptoed into Wyatt's camp and headed straight for the crate of sarsaparilla. Jo grabbed the crate and lifted it over her head. She was a superhero. She had no problem lifting gigantic things like boxes full of sarsaparilla. She carried the crate back to the woods and began pouring the contents of the bottles on the ground.

But what to replace it with? Jo looked at

Raymond, who was drooling like crazy. He gave
her a look that said, "I don't smell bacon, but that
doesn't mean I'm not thinking about it."

Dog drool, Jo thought. *Perfect!* She held one of
the empty bottles under Raymond's chin and filled
it to the brim with dog drool.

Jo reached for another empty bottle and held it
under Raymond's chin. Then she grabbed another.
And another. "Bacon," Jo whispered when her dog
started running out of slobber. "Pizza. Pork chops.
Hamburgers. Meatballs."

The more Jo named Raymond's favorite foods,
the more he drooled. Soon, all the sarsaparilla
bottles in the crate had become Raymond-slobber

bottles. Jo picked up the crate, walked it back into the camp, and laid it beside the sleeping Wyatt Burp. Then she stood back and yelled, "Wake up in the name of—"

"Wake up in the name of" sounded a whole lot like "Stop in the name of," and Jo never knew quite how to finish that sentence. Wake up in the name of a little girl in a cape? Wake up because I want to see your boss drink dog drool?

Jo started again. "Wake up in the name of—"

By this time every member of the Hole in the Head Gang was wide awake. And staring right at—

"It's the vampire!" Festus the Number Two Man yelled.

Vampire, thought Jo. *What vampire?* She looked around the camp. She was absolutely terrified of vampires. If there was a vampire in the area, she'd better say "Sponge cake" and get the heck out of there.

Raymond was also terrified of vampires. He gave Wyatt Burp a look that said, "Pardon me, but can I borrow your scarf?"

Wyatt was too busy reaching for a bottle of sarsaparilla. "Ha-ha!" he said. "I'll take care of you. And your little dog, too."

"My name is Raymond, not Too," Raymond's look said.

Wyatt took a huge swig of his favorite soft drink, then he reared back and gave it all he had.

19

Burp? What Burp?

Burp.

It was the tiniest burp in the long history of burping. Plus, it was the nastiest sarsaparilla Wyatt Burp had ever tasted. He took another drink and tried again.

Burp.

Festus the Number Two Man couldn't believe his ears. Or his nose. Where was the sound of thunder? Where was the smell of bacon? "Boss? Don't tell

me you lost your ability to burp." He pointed to Jo and Raymond. "Vampires. Remember?"

Jo was no vampire. She did, however, have a great Knuckle Sandwich. And a pretty good Russian Toe hold and Siberian Ear Tweak, for that matter.

Time to go to work.

Smack!

Pow!

Splat!

Soon every member of the Hole in the Head Gang was lying on the ground with a black eye.

All except Wyatt Burp, who was still drinking bottle after bottle of dog drool and trying to burp.

Burp. "Curses!" he said. "What happened to my burp?"

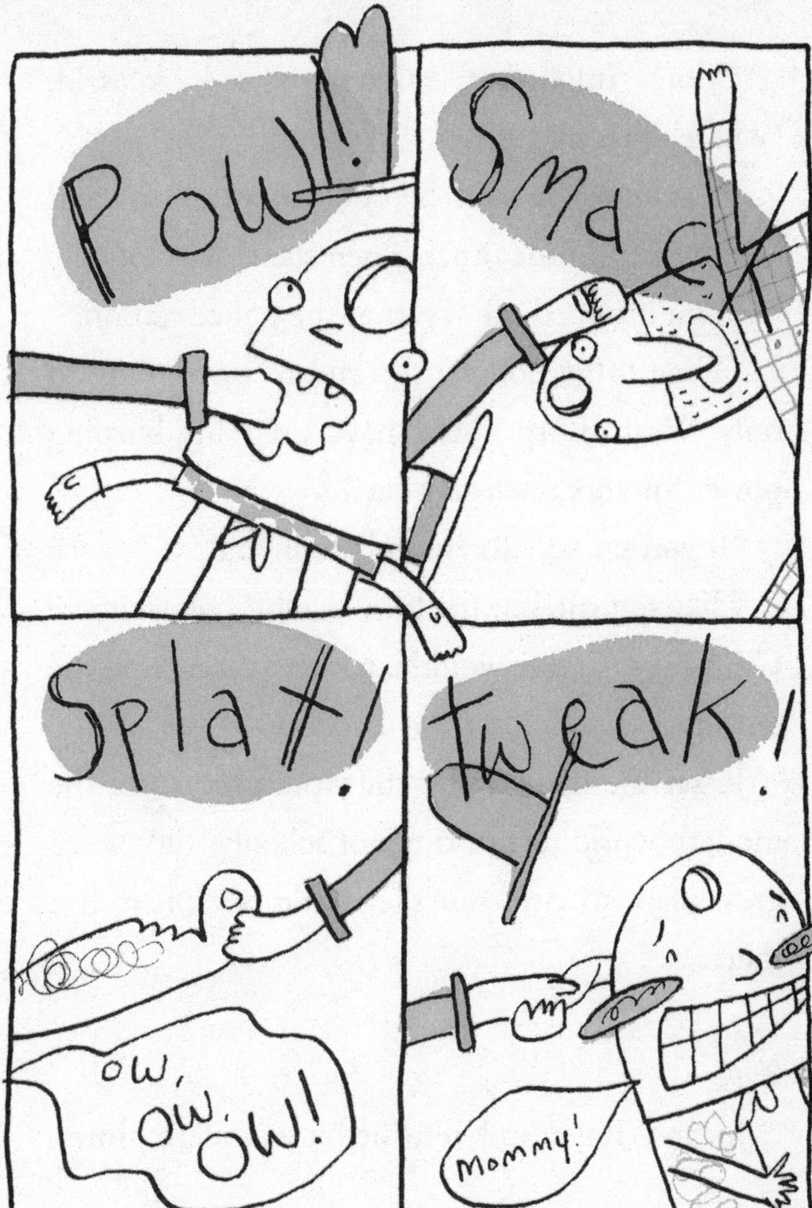
Pow!
Smack!
Splatt!
OW, OW, OW!
tweak!
Mommy!

"More important," Raymond's look said, "where's that bacon?"

Jo Schmo grabbed her dog in one arm and Wyatt Burp in the other. Then she flew across the bay and dropped off Wyatt at the police station.

"Time to go home," she said to Raymond. "If only Wyatt Burp could have used his burping power for good instead of evil."

"If you say so," Raymond's look said.

They returned to the little patch of grass where Crimshaw Avenue would later be, and entered the outhouse . . . uh . . . time machine.

Jo set the dial so that she would return to the modern world just in time for school; 1849 was a great place to visit, but she wouldn't want to live there.

Zap!

Jo and Raymond returned to modern times.

But little did they know that Gertrude McSlime and Betty Sludgefoot were waiting for them. As Jo sped along in the Schmomobile, she had no idea that there was a wrecking ball with her name on it. To be honest, there was no name at all on the wrecking ball. It was just this huge, heavy black thing, but you get the idea.

"Here she comes!" Gertrude said.

Gertrude pulled a few levers, and a gigantic wrecking ball weighing thousands of pounds came swooshing through the air in the direction of Jo Schmo and her little dog, too.

But Jo heard the swooshing. She stopped just in time. She turned toward the wrecking ball, balled up her fist, and—

Pow!

The wrecking ball collided with Jo Schmo's Knuckle Sandwich, and who do you think won?

Jo Schmo, of course.

"Curses!"
yelled Gertrude
McSlime.

"Yes, curses!"
yelled Betty Sludgefoot.
"Where are those water
balloons?"

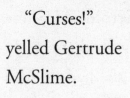

wheeee

Back at school, Jo Schmo was feeling pretty good. She'd just captured the notorious outlaw Wyatt Burp and got the best of a wrecking ball weighing thousands of pounds. Life was good.

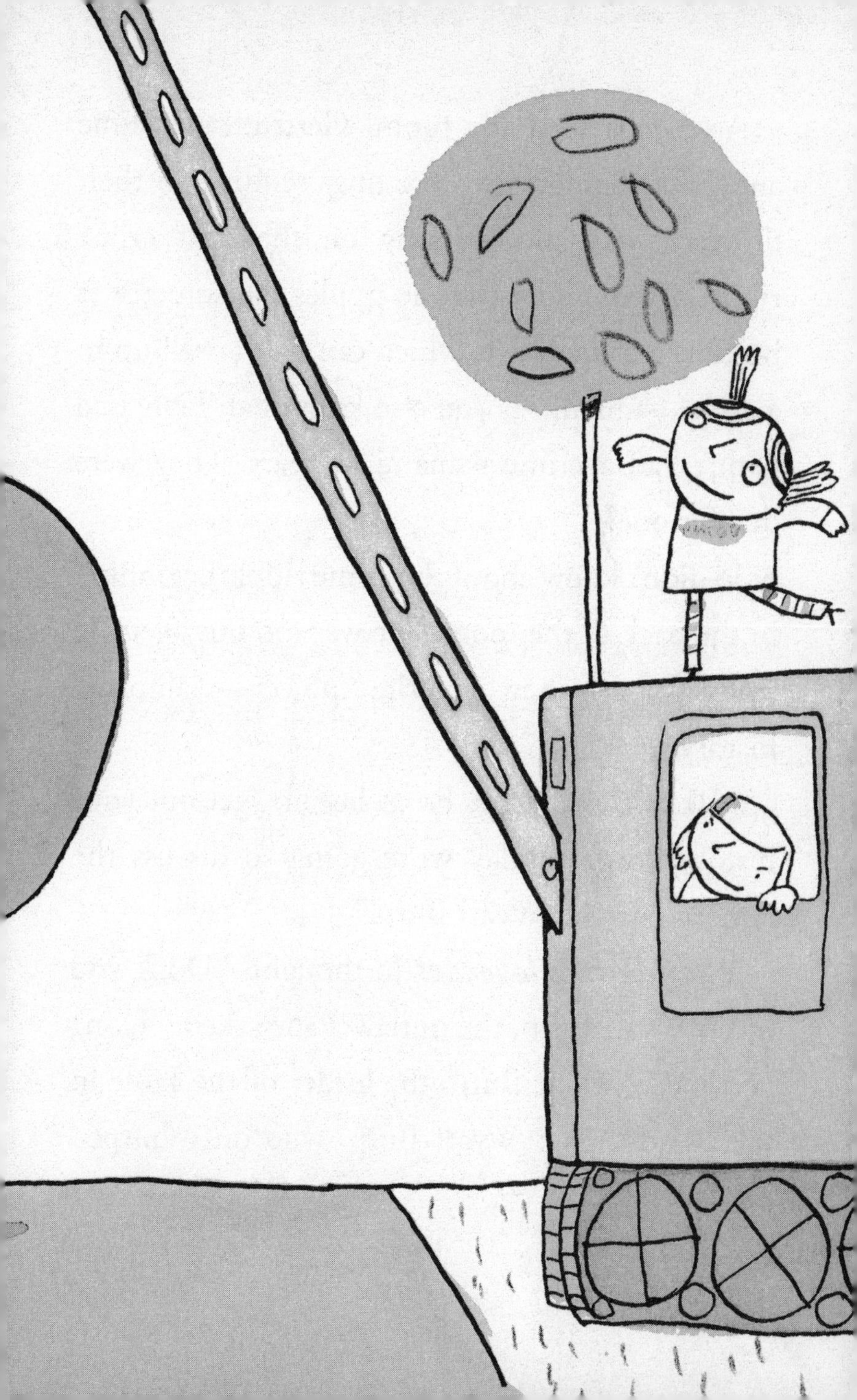

At the back of the room, Gertrude McSlime and Betty Sludgefoot were busy sending Jo their dirtiest looks and working on the next crime ripple. As you know, crime ripples can sometimes become a crime wave, which can work itself up to a crime tsunami. As you also know, San Francisco hadn't had a crime tsunami in years. They were due for one.

Jo didn't know about the crime ripple beginning in the back of the room. She was too busy getting ready for her new favorite subject—California history.

"Okay, class," Mrs. Freep began, "get out your history books. Today we're going to discuss the famous lawman Wyatt Burp."

Wyatt Burp a lawman? Jo thought. "Don't you mean Wyatt Burp, the outlaw?" she asked. "Don't you mean Wyatt Burp, the leader of the Hole in the Head Gang? Wyatt Burp, who once burped the doors off a bank vault and the smell of what he'd had for breakfast lingered for days?"

"That's exactly who I mean," Mrs. Freep said. "But after an encounter with a miniature vampire, Mr. Burp changed his ways. When he got out of jail, he decided to use his burping power for good instead of evil."

"Well, what do you know about that?" Jo said to herself. She turned around and saw the evil stares of Betty Sludgefoot and Gertrude McSlime, but Jo didn't care. She was now part of the California history books, and how many fourth-graders can say that?

Time travel sure was complicated.

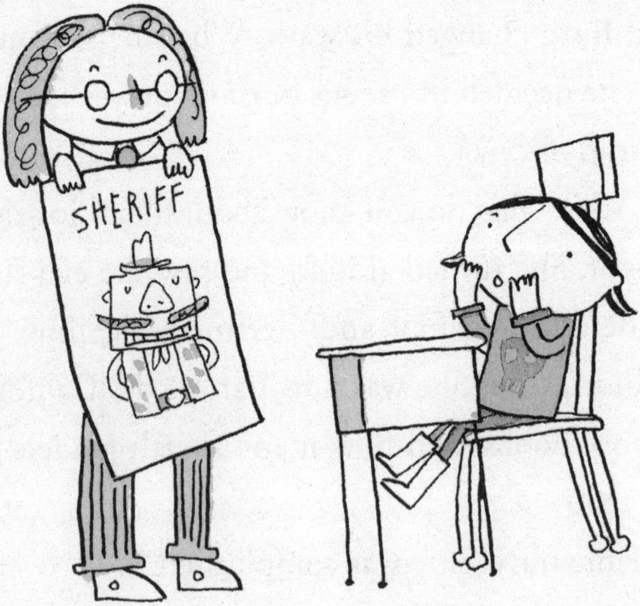
SHERIFF